modern readers — stage 3

A Christmas Tale

Eduardo Amos
Elisabeth Prescher

2nd edition

Richmond

© EDUARDO AMOS, ELISABETH PRESCHER, 2005

 Richmond

Diretoria: *Paul Berry*
Gerência editorial: *Sandra Possas*
Coordenação de *bureau: Américo Jesus*
Coordenação de revisão: *Estevam Vieira Lédo Jr.*
Coordenação de produção gráfica: *André Monteiro, Maria de Lourdes Rodrigues*
Coordenação de produção industrial: *Wilson Troque*

Projeto editorial: *Véra Regina A. Maselli*

Assistência editorial: *Gabriela Peixoto Vilanova*
Consultoria de língua inglesa: *Marylou Bielenstein*
Preparação: *Margaret Presser*
Revisão: *Elaine Cristina del Nero*
Projeto gráfico de miolo e capa: *Ricardo Van Steen Comunicações e Propaganda Ltda./Oliver Fuchs*
Edição de arte: *Claudiner Corrêa Filho*
Ilustrações de miolo e capa: *Studio Zig-Zag*
Tratamento de imagens: *Fabio N. Precendo, Rubens M. Rodrigues*
Diagramação: *Tânia Balsini*
Pré-impressão: *Hélio P. de Souza Filho, Marcio H. Kamoto*
Impressão e acabamento: Gráfica Printi
Cód: 12044858
Lote: 805635

Dados Internacionais de Catalogação na Publicação (CIP)
(Câmara Brasileira do Livro, SP, Brasil)

Amos, Eduardo.
 A Christmas tale / Eduardo Amos, Elisabeth
Prescher. — 2. ed. — São Paulo :
Moderna, 2005. — (Modern readers ; stage 3)

 1. Inglês (Ensino fundamental) I. Prescher,
Elisabeth. II. Título. III. Série.

04-8851   CDD-372.652

Índices para catálogo sistemático:
1. Inglês : Ensino fundamental   372.652

ISBN 85-16-04485-8

Reprodução proibida. Art. 184 do Código Penal e Lei 9.610 de 19 de fevereiro de 1998.

Todos os direitos reservados.

RICHMOND
SANTILLANA EDUCAÇÃO LTDA.
Rua Padre Adelino, 758, 3º andar — Belenzinho
São Paulo — SP — Brasil — CEP 03303-904
www.richmond.com.br
2025
Impresso no Brasil

Profound transformations occurred in London in the first half of the nineteenth century.

Electricity brought light to the dark nights of the city. The steam engine stimulated the development of factories. The textile industry alone employed thousands of people. Prosperity and poverty existed side by side.

Those were the days of the Industrial Revolution.

On the poor side of town, across the bridge, lived the workers. They had large families and small, cold houses. Their young children played in the unpaved streets among dogs, cats, and rats.

It was past eight when Joshua Deen arrived home from work. He was usually very tired at that time. He had to work hard to support his wife and five children. Money was short and everyone in the family had to do something to help. Mrs. Deen did embroidery. Alma, the oldest daughter, baked cookies and did the housework. Julian was only thirteen. He worked at the factory with his father. Alan was ten. He did odd jobs and looked after his younger sister Ann and brother Victor.

    The days were long for Joshua and Julian Deen — they worked sixteen hours a day from Monday to Saturday.

    Working conditions were harsh. The machinery was noisy and dangerous. The temperature in the factory was high because of the steam engines. It was difficult to breathe there. Joshua was always coughing and Julian had a constant cold.

Alan didn't want to work in the factories. He knew it was hard. He knew they paid very little to young children. He knew the workers were always sick. But he wanted to do something to help his family.

He did some jobs downtown — he delivered newspapers, and did some gardening. He also sold the cookies that Alma baked.

Alan delivered his mother's embroidery too. He was glad every time she sent him to Chelsea. That was the rich part of London. Everything was beautiful there — the houses, the people, the carriages. And... Mmmmmmm! the smells were wonderful.

"This house smells like bread!" he said to himself in front of a red brick house.

"This one smells like apple pie!" he said as he walked around the corner.

"What's this now? Perfume?!"

One cold morning he was delivering a package at an old lady's house.

"Thank you, Alan," said the lady. "Your mother's work is really beautiful! Wish her a Merry Christmas!"

"Christmas?!" he asked himself as he walked away. "Oh! That's right! It's Christmas time."

He wanted to buy a present for his family. He wanted them to have a Merry Christmas, but how?

He delivered embroidery all morning. Then, he sold cookies downtown in the afternoon.

"I made good money today," he thought. "But I can't buy any presents."

He knew his father and his brother Julian needed medicine. His mother needed candles, and Victor had no shoes for the winter.

And he knew there were only three more days until Christmas.

The next morning Alan woke up very early. He kissed his mother and left home as usual. He had something in mind that morning — he was going to find a Christmas present for his family.

He worked all day. Then, late in the afternoon, he went downtown.

The streets were crowded. There were people shopping everywhere.

Alan went to the stalls and bazaars. He looked in the shop windows. Everything was so beautiful... and so expensive!

"I have to find something," he thought.

He walked around the stalls and shops all afternoon but he didn't see anything that he could buy. It was dark and many shops were closing. There were few people in the streets at that time.

Alan was sad, cold, and very hungry. He had to go back home.

"Oh, no!" he said to himself. "I was sure I was going to find a Christmas present for my family!"

He was walking home disconsolately when something in a dustbin caught his eye.

He crossed the street, looked around, and took the object from the dustbin. He wrapped it in his coat and hurried home.

Late that night, the Deens' house was silent.
Everyone was asleep. Alan took his find from under the pillow, unwrapped it, and examined it. It was an old lamp.
"What a pity it isn't magic!" he thought while he was cleaning it. Then, he had an idea. "If I put a candle in it, it will make a nice candleholder! It'll light our Christmas Eve!"
Alan was very proud of his idea and slept happily.

The twenty-fourth of December was even colder.
Alan left home very early to do his usual jobs. When he was crossing the bridge, an announcement caught his attention.

Alan's heart beat faster. His eyes opened wider.
He ran back home and got the lamp.
Then, he grabbed Ann and Victor and hurried to Baker Street.

Sir Holmes was very happy to have the lamp back in his antique shop.

"Thank you, my boy!" he said. "Here is your reward. And Merry Christmas!!!"

Alan, Victor, and Ann spent the whole afternoon shopping. They were the happiest people in London that afternoon.

When night came, the Deens were sitting around the table. It was their first real Christmas dinner.

"I'm so glad Santa Claus came to our house this year," said Ann.

"Yes, darling," said Mrs. Deen. "We're all very happy."

"It's difficult to come to this side of town," said Joshua.

"Well," said Alan. "It's hard to cross the bridge on a sleigh! Merry Christmas!!!"

KEY WORDS

The meaning of each word corresponds to its use in the context of the story (see page number 00)

across (4) através
also (8) também
among (4) entre
announcement (18) anúncio
antique shop (19) antiquário
anything (16) algo
around (11) ao redor
arrive (5) chegar
asleep (17) adormecido
bake (5) assar
bazaar (14) bazar
beat (18) pulsar
bread (11) pão
breathe (6) respirar
brick (11) tijolo
bridge (4) ponte
buy (12) comprar
candle (13) vela
candleholder (17) castiçal
carriage (10) carruagem
caught his eye (16) chamou sua atenção
century (3) século
Christmas Eve (17) véspera de Natal
clean (17) limpar
coat (16) casaco
cold (4) frio
cooky (5) biscoito
corner (11) esquina; canto
cough (6) tossir

cross (16) cruzar, atravessar
crowded (14) lotado
dark (3) escuro
deliver (8) entregar
development (3) desenvolvimento
disconsolately (16) desconsoladamente
downtown (8) centro da cidade
dustbin (16) lata de lixo
early (14) cedo
embroidery (5) bordado
employ (3) empregar
engine (3) máquina; motor
even (18) mesmo
every (10) cada
everyone (5) todos
everything (10) tudo
everywhere (14) todo lugar
factory (3) fábrica
fast (18) rápido
few (16) poucos
find (14) achar
gardening (8) jardinagem
grab (18) agarrar
half (3) metade
happily (17) alegremente
hard (5) duro, difícil
harsh (6) severo
heart (18) coração

high (6) alto
housework (5) trabalho
  doméstico
hungry (16) faminto
hurry (16) apressar-se
job (5) trabalho
kiss (14) beijar
late (14) tarde
light (3) luz; iluminar
live (4) viver
look after (5) cuidar
machinery (6) maquinário
mind (14) mente
need (13) precisar
next (14) próximo
noisy (6) barulhento
occur (3) ocorrer
open (18) abrir
package (12) pacote
part (10) parte
pie (11) torta
pillow (17) travesseiro
play (4) brincar
poor (4) pobre
poverty (3) pobreza
proud (17) orgulhoso
real (12) real
reward (19) recompensa
rich (10) rico
shoe (13) sapato
shop (16) loja

shop window (14) vitrina
short (5) curto
sick (8) doente
side (3) lado
sleigh (20) trenó
smell (11) cheiro
something (5) algo
spend (19) gastar, passar
stall (14) barraca
steam (3) vapor
support (5) manter
then (13) então
thousand (4) mil
town (4) cidade
under (17) sob
unpaved (4) não-pavimentado
until (13) até
usual (5) usual
want (8) querer
while (17) enquanto
whole (19) inteiro
wide (18) largo
wish (12) desejar
wrap (16) embrulhar
young (4) jovem

Expressions

What a pity! (17) Que pena!
Merry Christmas! (12) Feliz Natal!
That's right. (12) Certo.

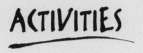

Vocabulary exercises

A. Match the columns. Find the synonyms.

1. occurred
2. usually
3. hard
4. only
5. constant
6. wonderful
7. rich
8. sure
9. everyone
10. dustbin

( ) just
( ) certain
( ) happened
( ) marvelous
( ) garbage can
( ) difficult
( ) continuous
( ) everybody
( ) generally
( ) wealthy

B. Choose the best word for each blank.

> wish   employed   support   looked after   breathe
> knew   sent   bought   delivered   rushed

1. The government is going to _____ the educational project.
2. Open the windows, please! I can't _____ in this closed room.
3. She _____ my name but she didn't remember my address.
4. I'm writing to you because I want to _____ you a Happy Birthday.
5. The newspaper boy _____ the newspaper very late yesterday. We didn't receive it until 6 o'clock.
6. They _____ a new sofa because the old one was falling apart.
7. Our company _____ twenty workers last year.

23

8. We _____ to the club after school. We had an important game to play.

9. Diana _____ our children from 3 to 6 yesterday while we went shopping.

10. Carol _____ us a postcard from Paris.

Comprehension exercises

C. Choose the correct alternative.

1. Joshua and Julian worked
   a) six days a week.
   b) six hours a day.
   c) in an antique shop.

2. Why didn't Mrs. Deen do the housework?
   a) Because she had to do her embroidery.
   b) Because she worked in a factory.
   c) Because she worked downtown.

3. What did Alan want to do when he knew it was Christmas time?
   a) He wanted to buy a present for his brother.
   b) He wanted to buy a present for his family.
   c) He wanted to buy a present for his girlfriend.

4. Why couldn't Alan buy a present?
   a) Because he didn't work.
   b) Because he didn't find anything.
   c) Because everything was very expensive and he didn't have enough money.

5. What did Alan find in a dustbin?
   a) An announcement.
   b) An old lamp.
   c) A candleholder.

6. What did Alan buy with the reward he received?
   a) He bought a present for himself.
   b) He bought food and drink for a real Christmas dinner.
   c) He bought a lot of toys.